MORE!

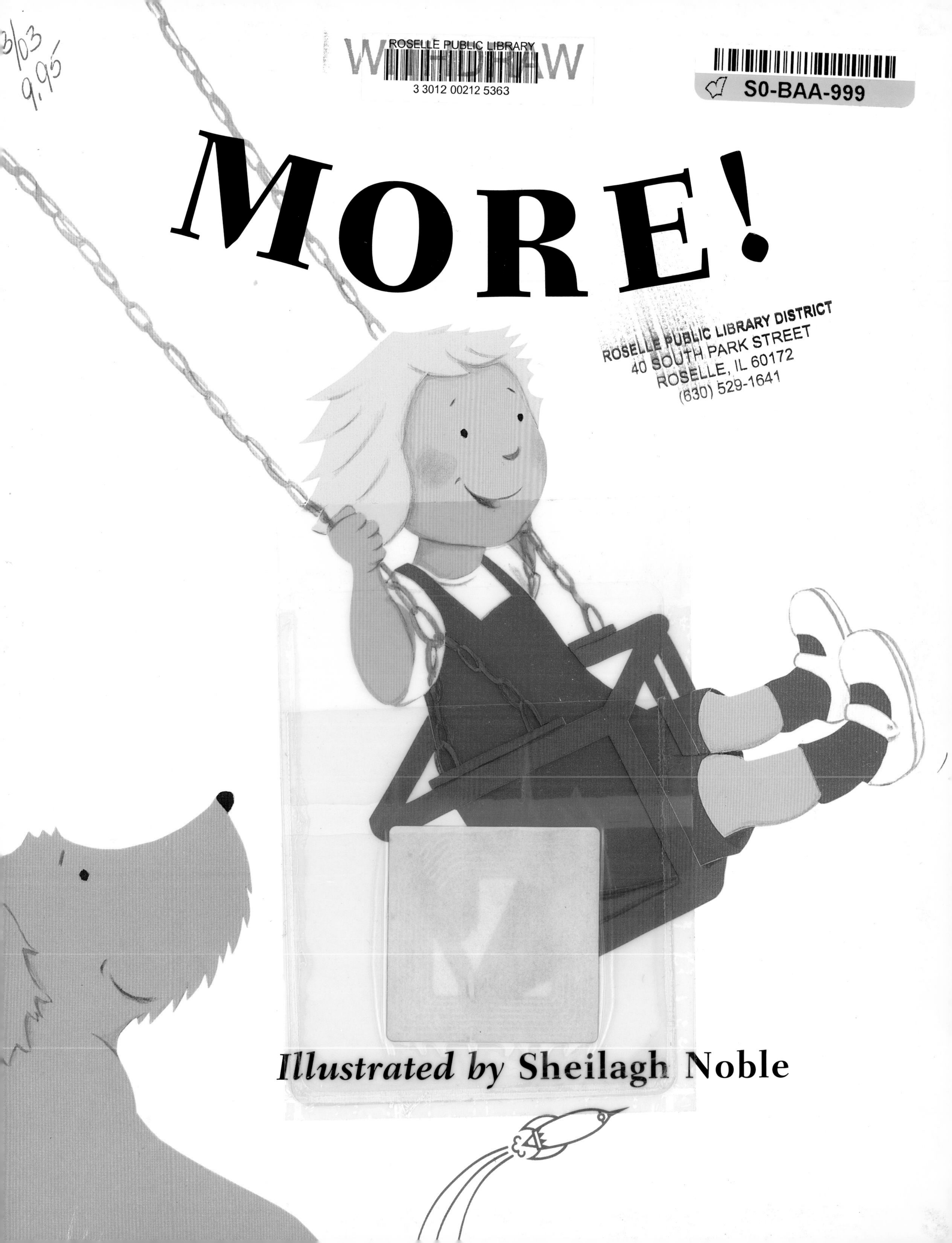

Illustrated by **Sheilagh Noble**

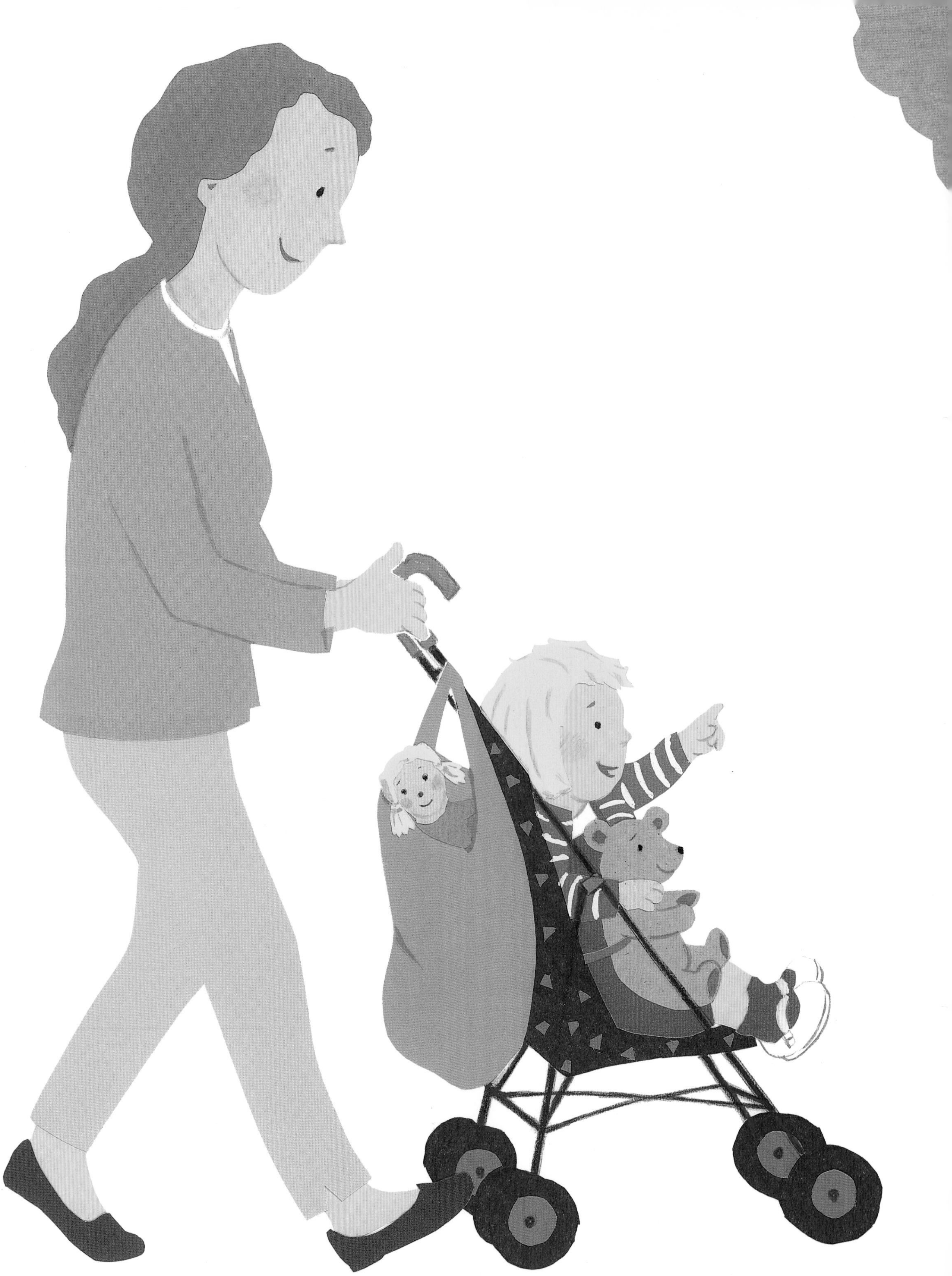

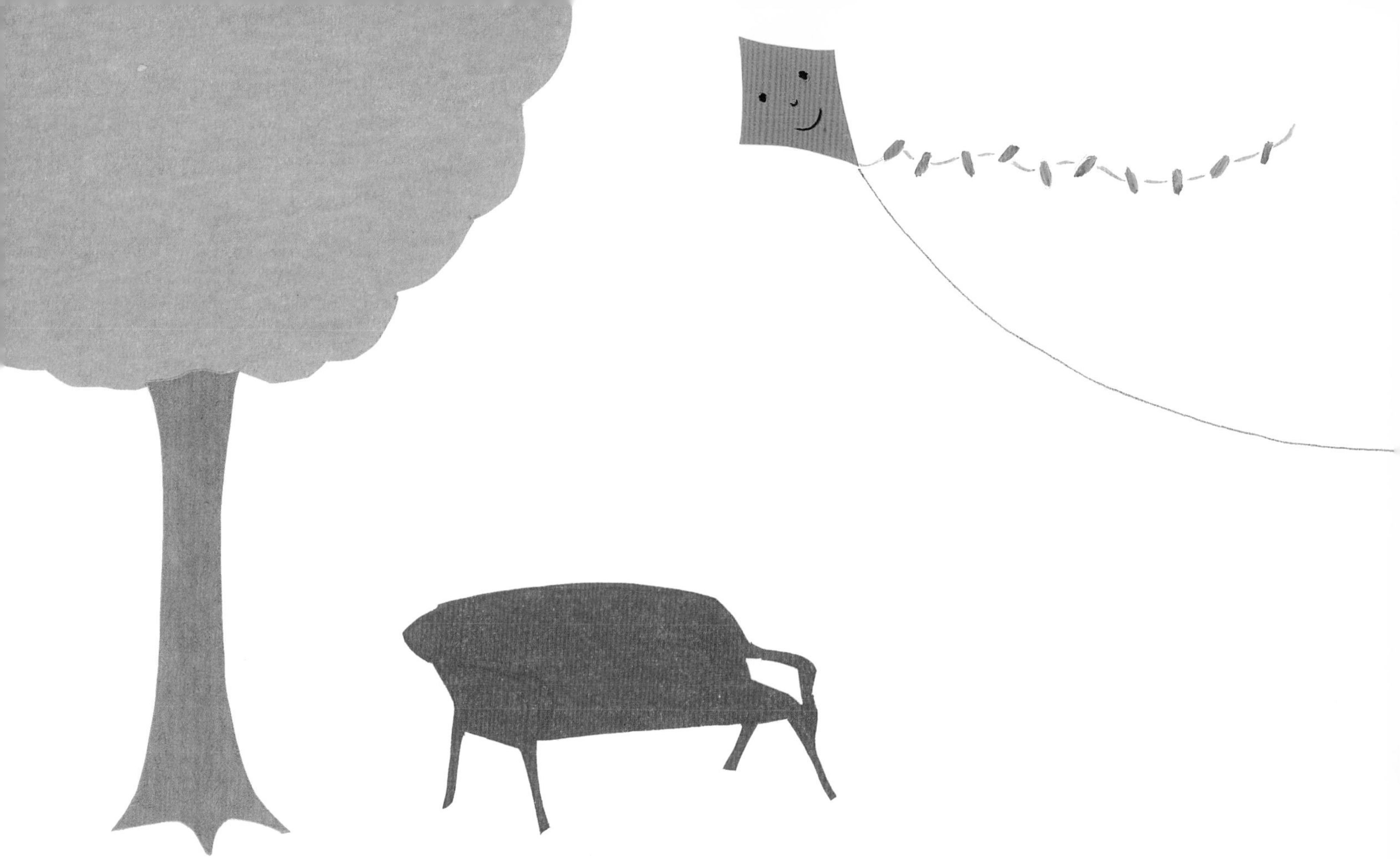

Look!

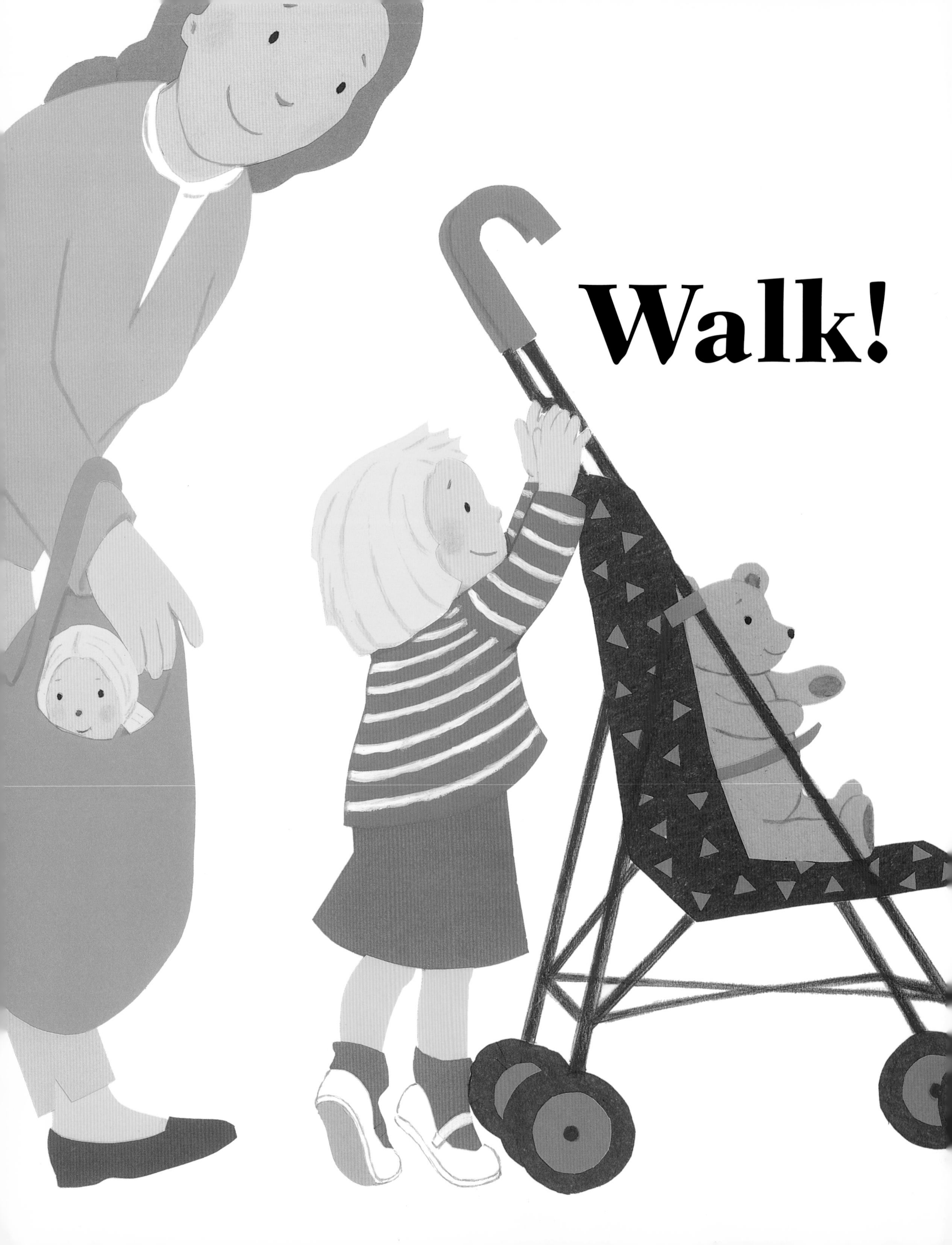

Walk!

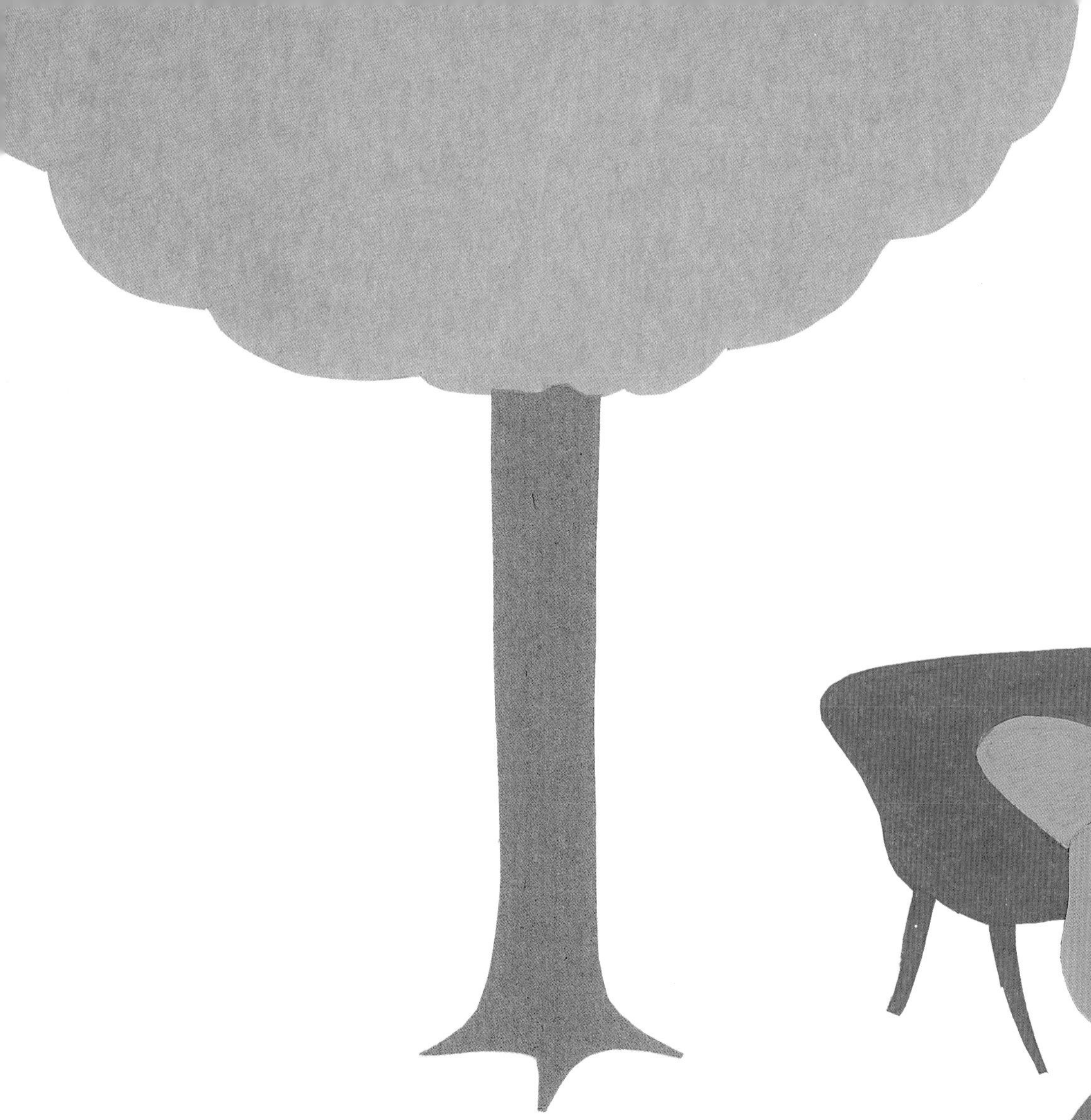

Hi!

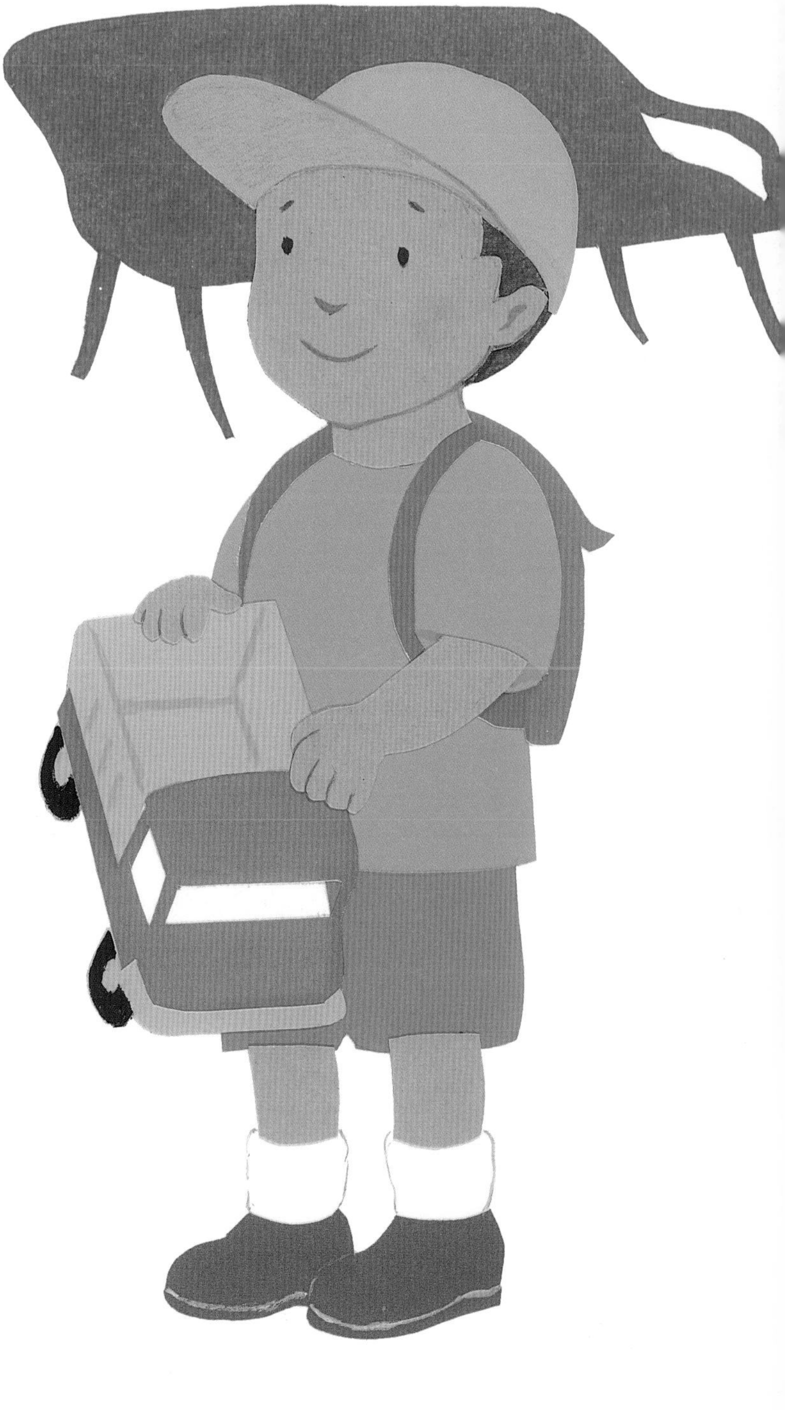

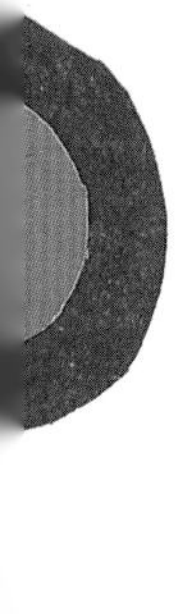

Chatter

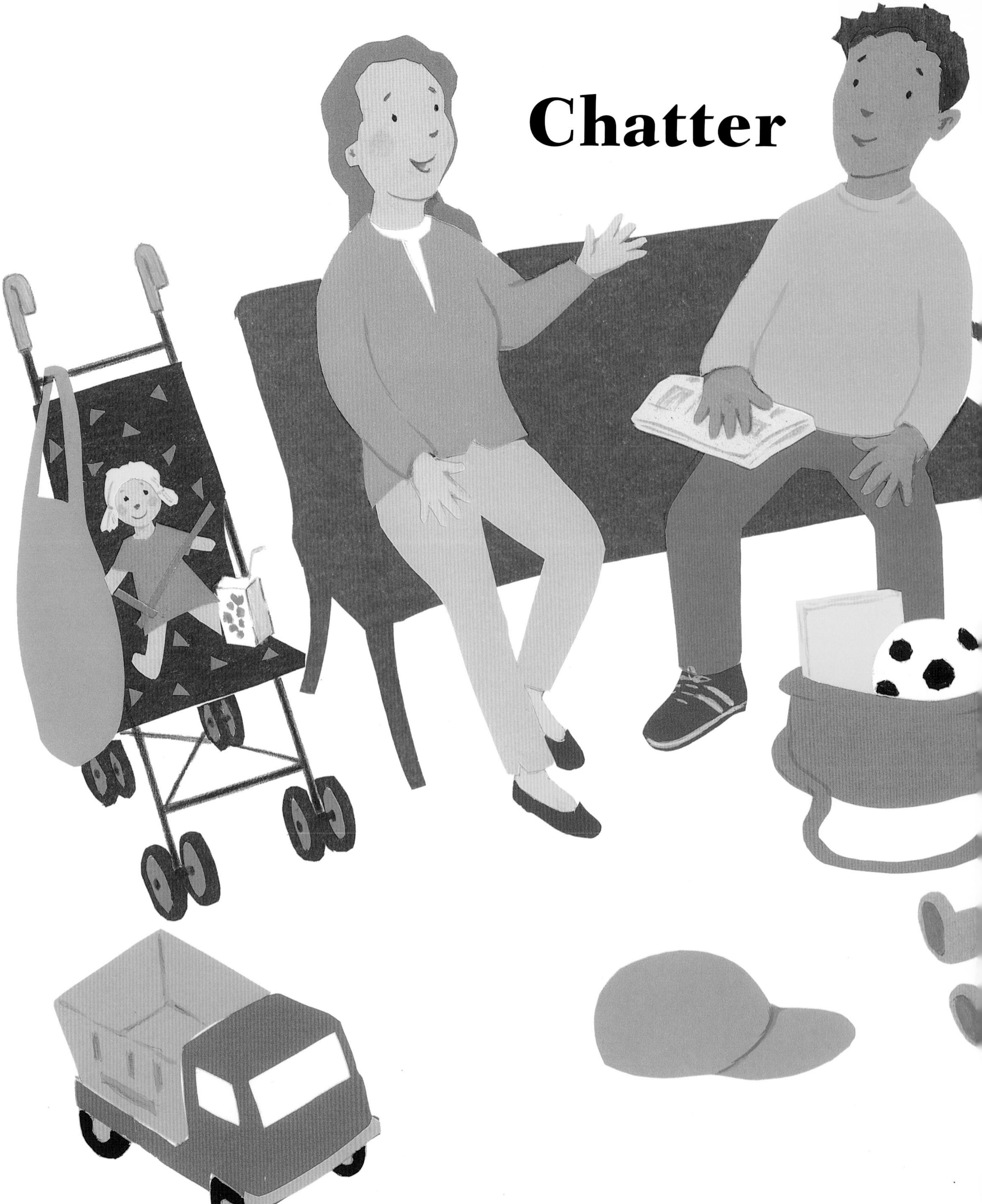

Chatter

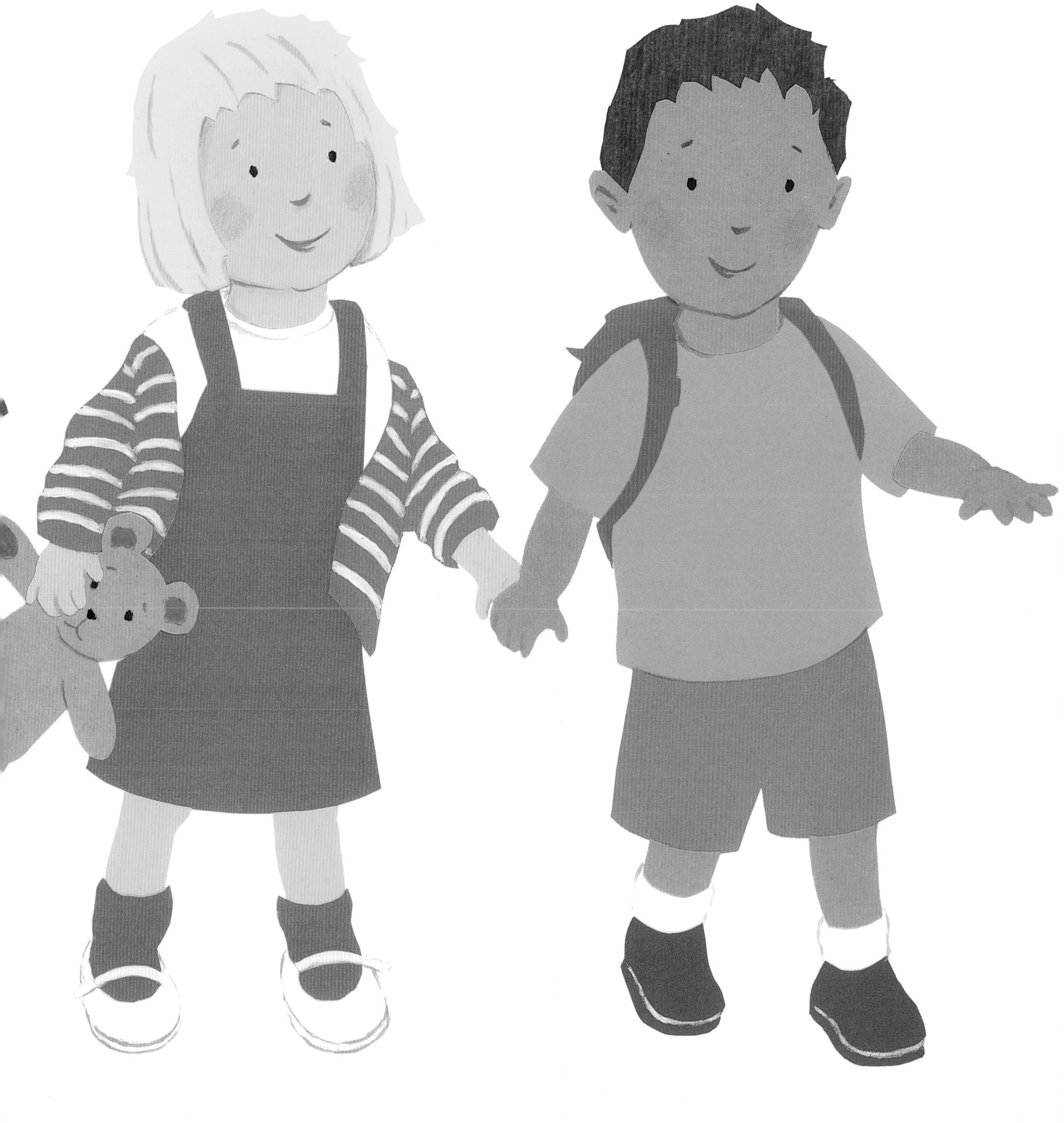

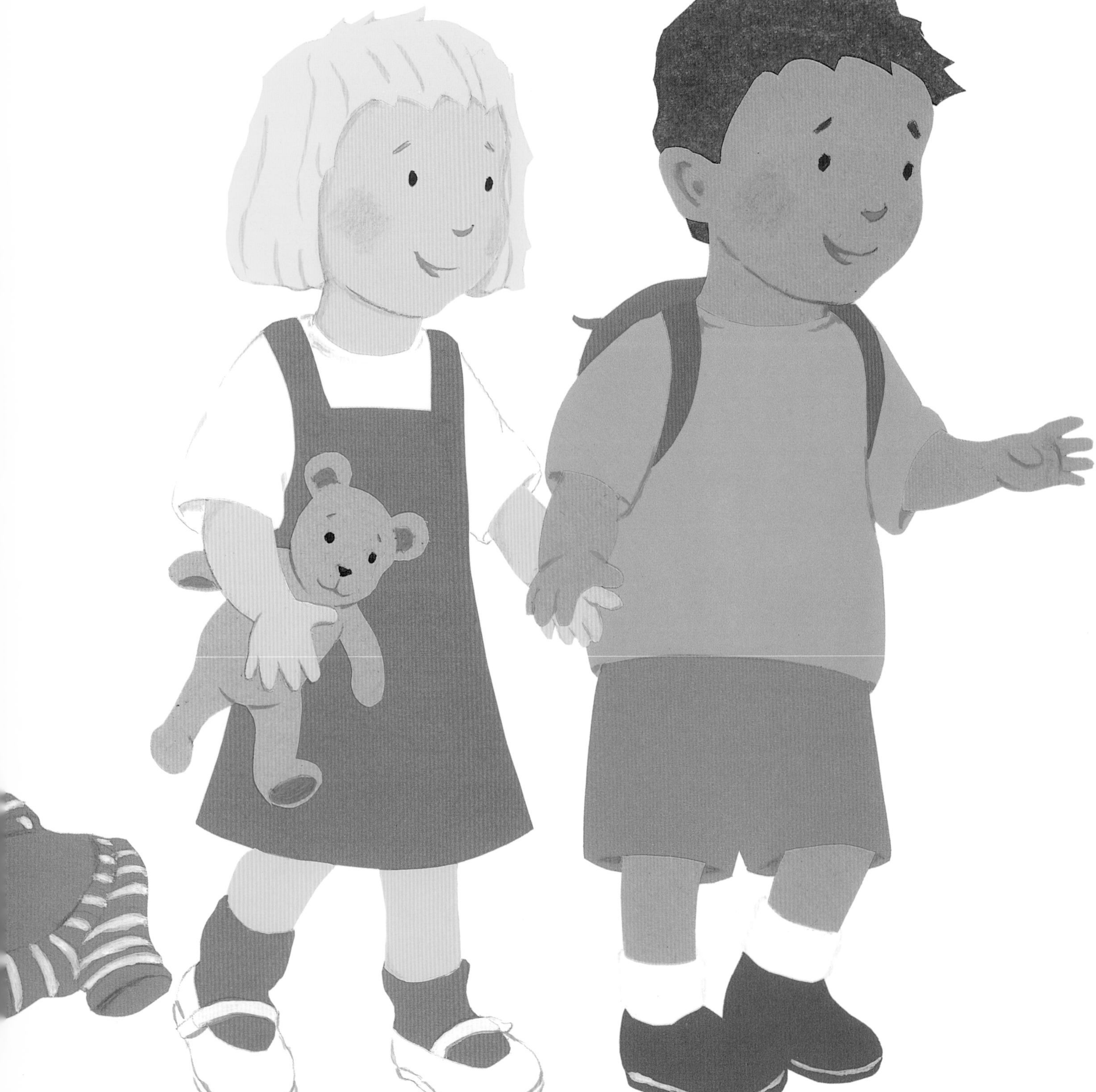

Duck!

Quack!

Quack!

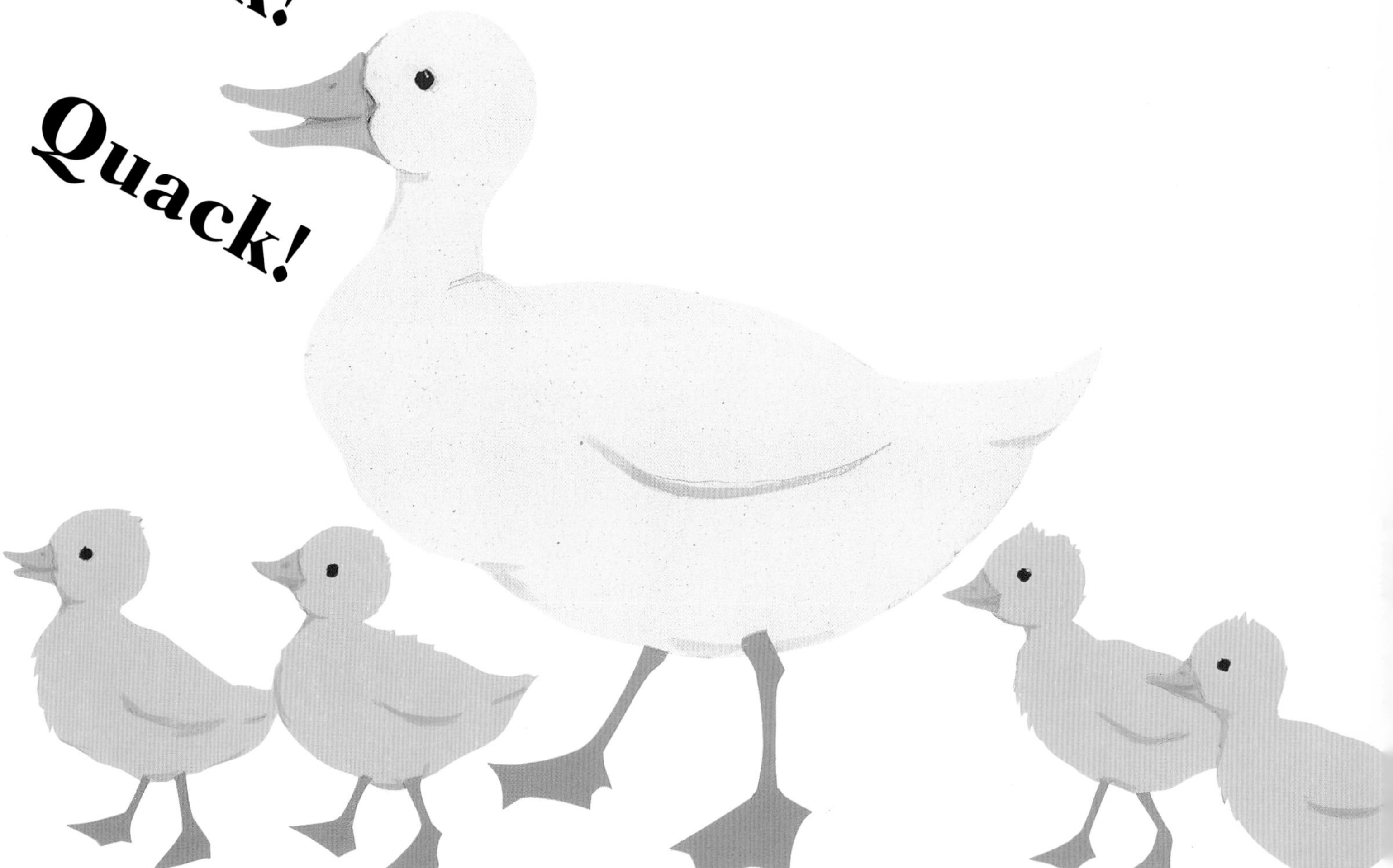

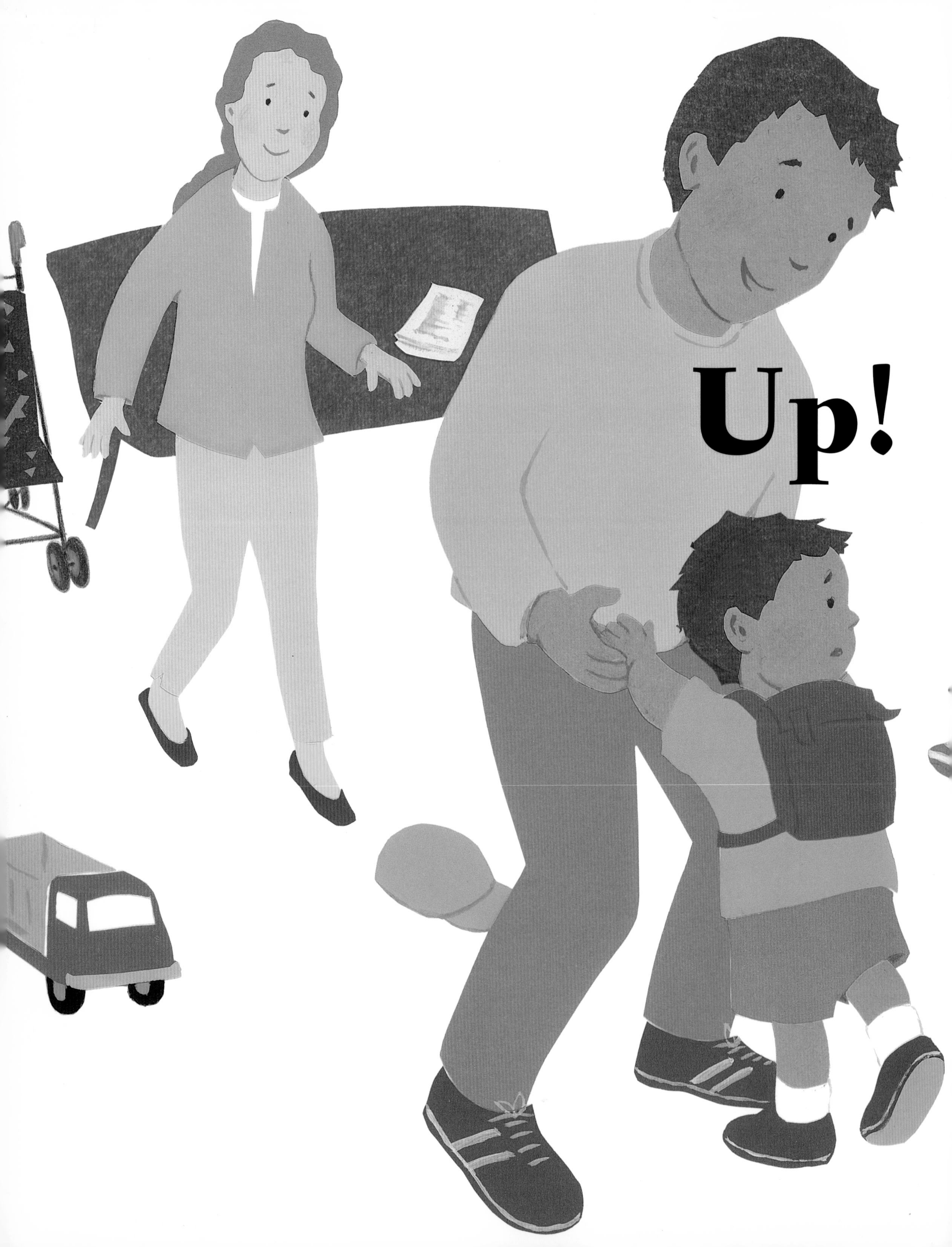

Up!

Dog!

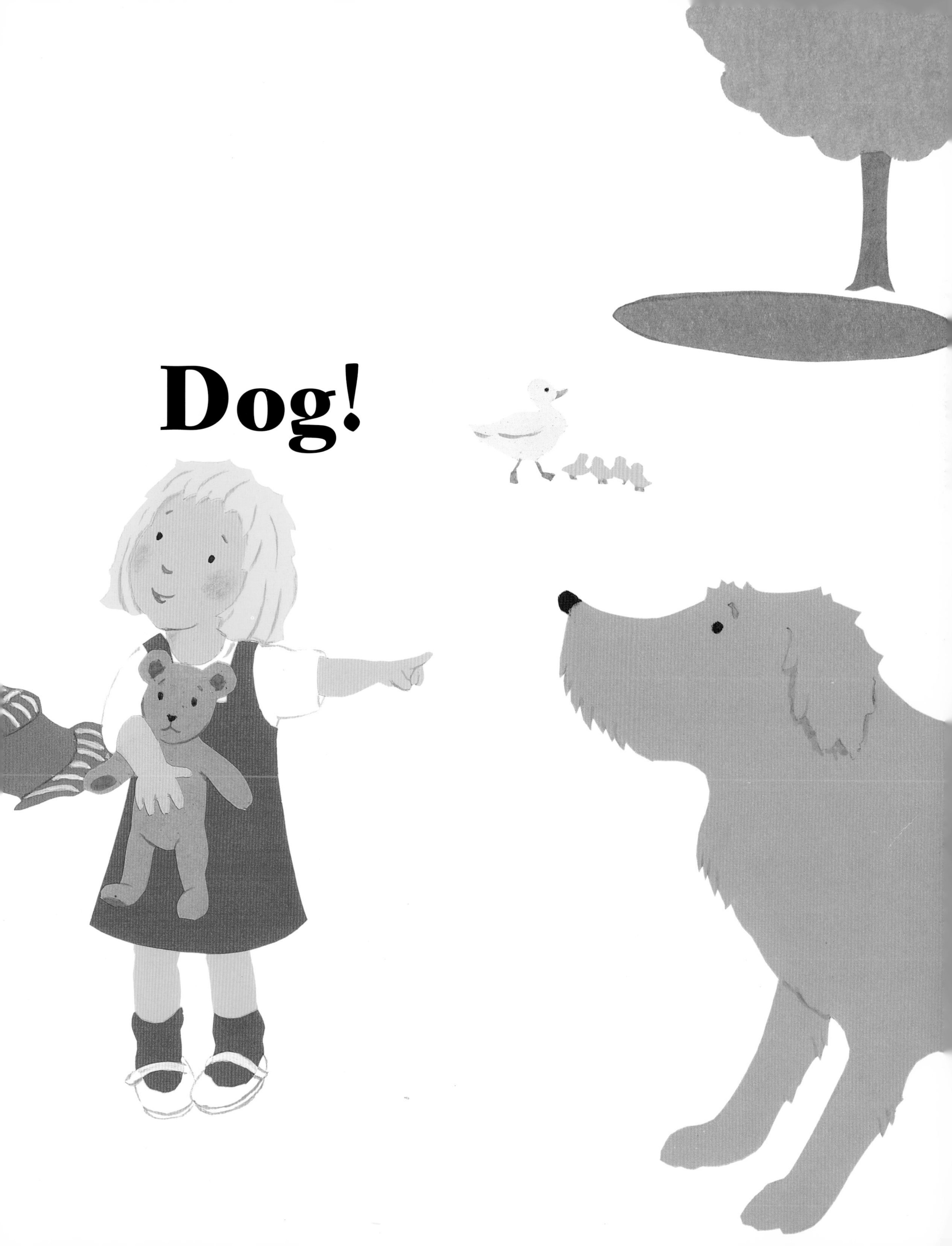

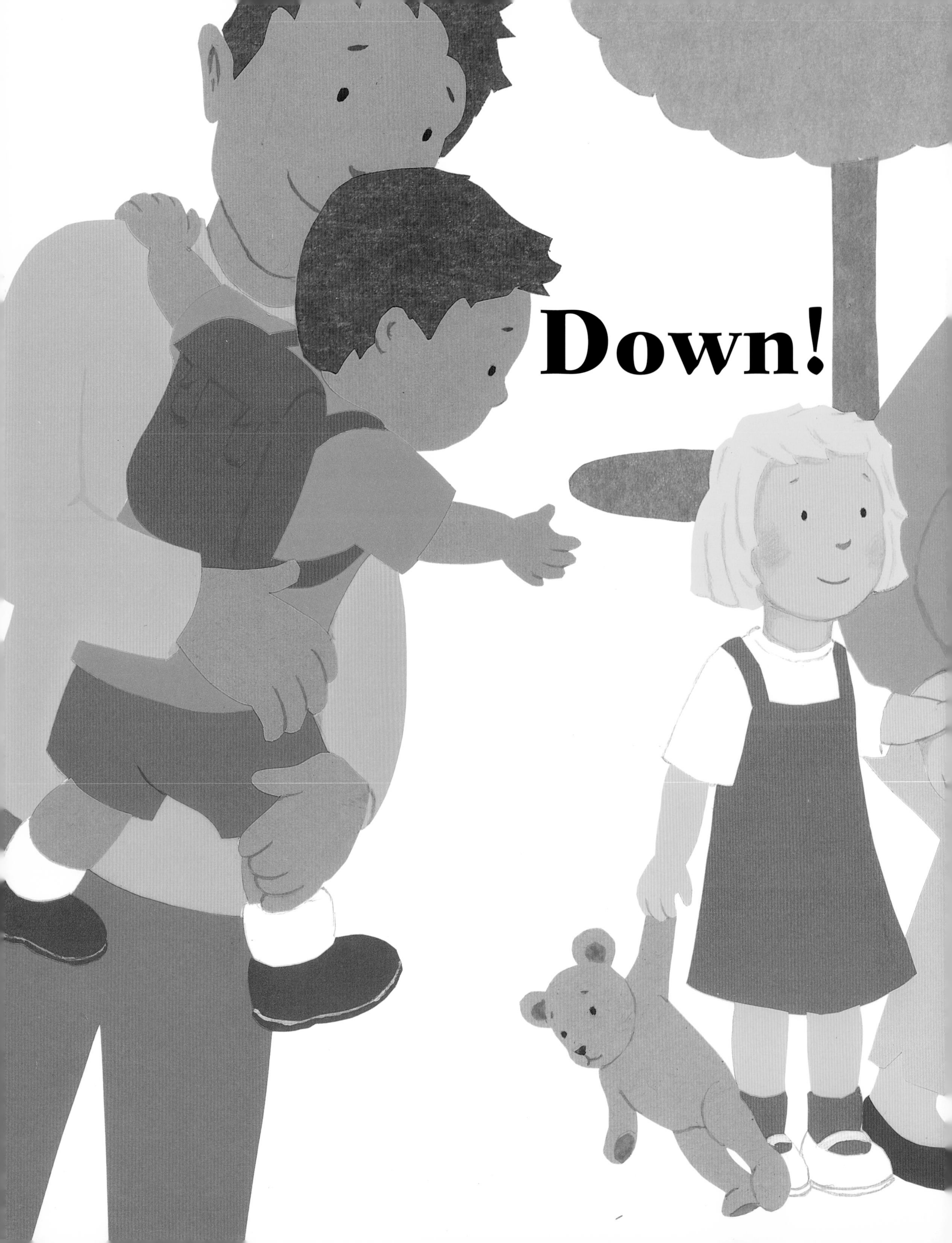

Down!

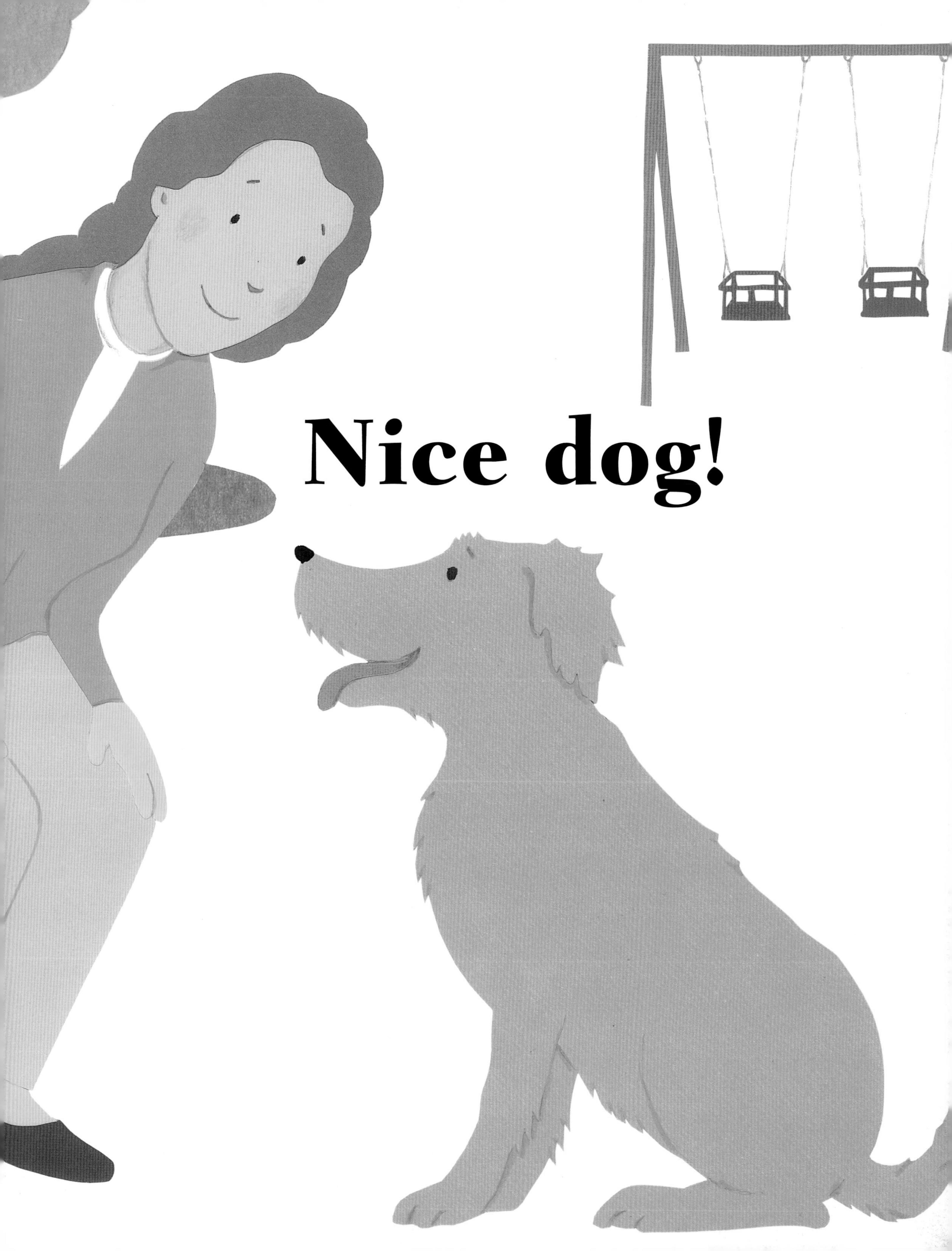

Nice dog!

Swings!

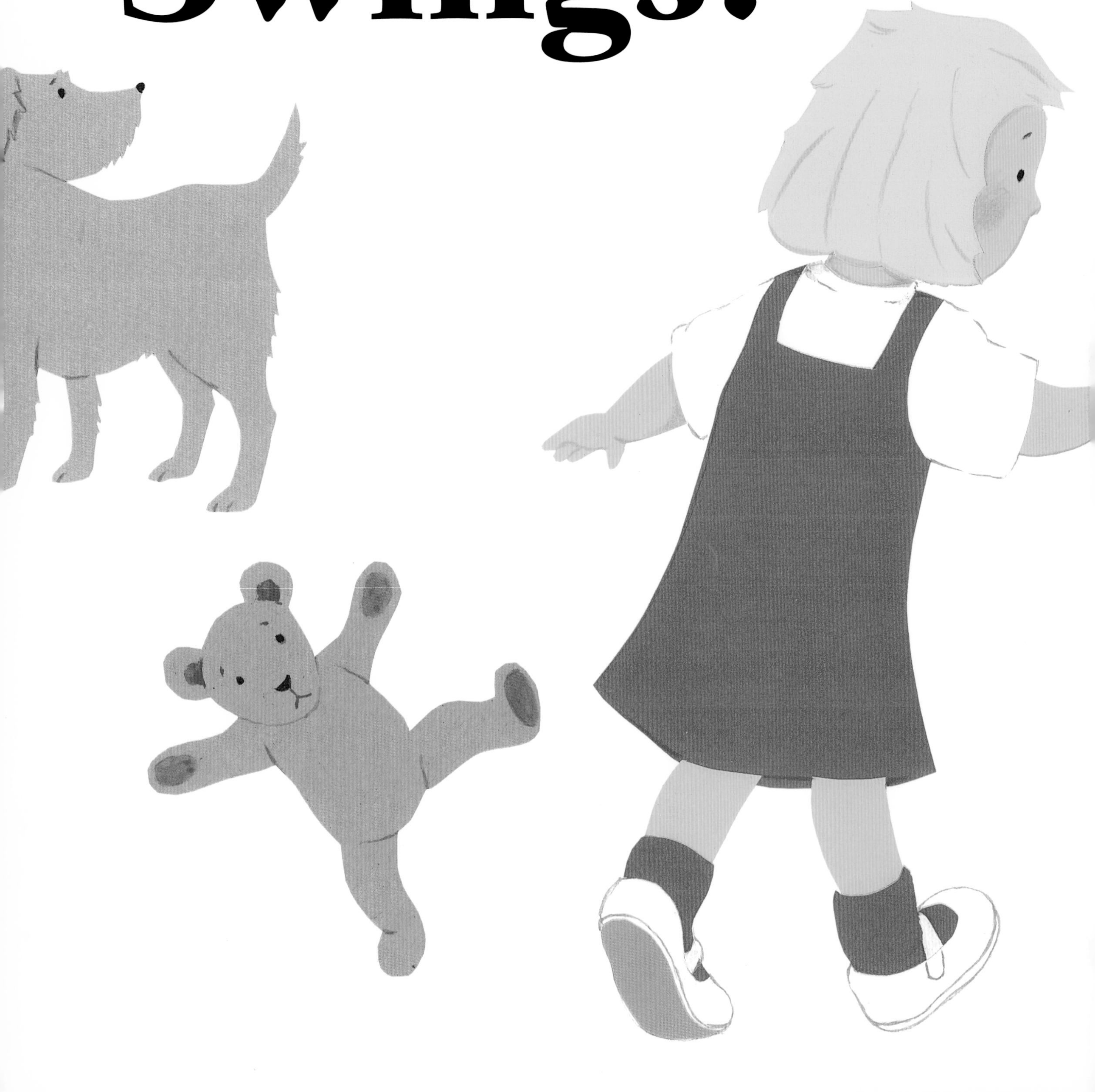

Come on!

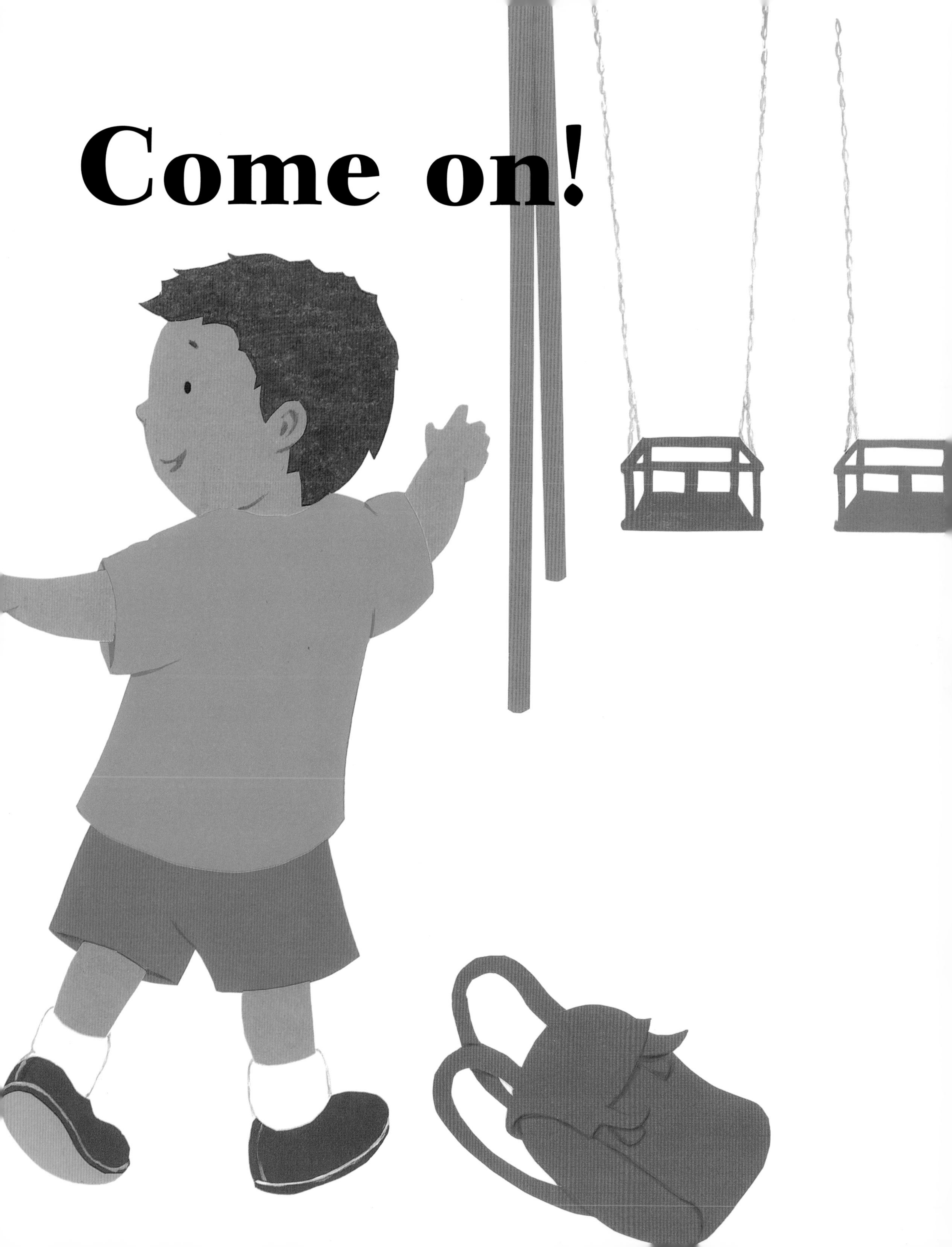

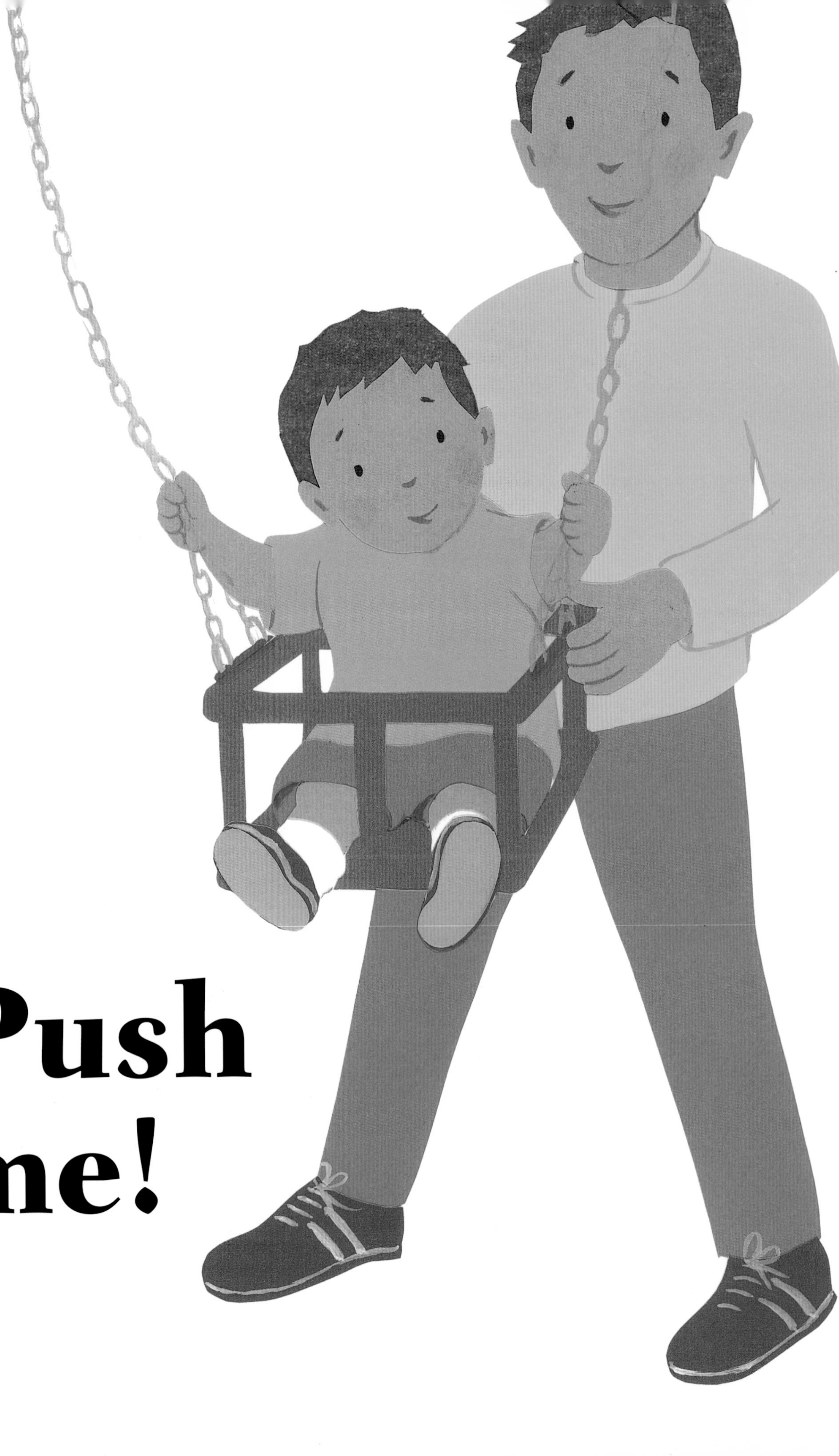

Push me!

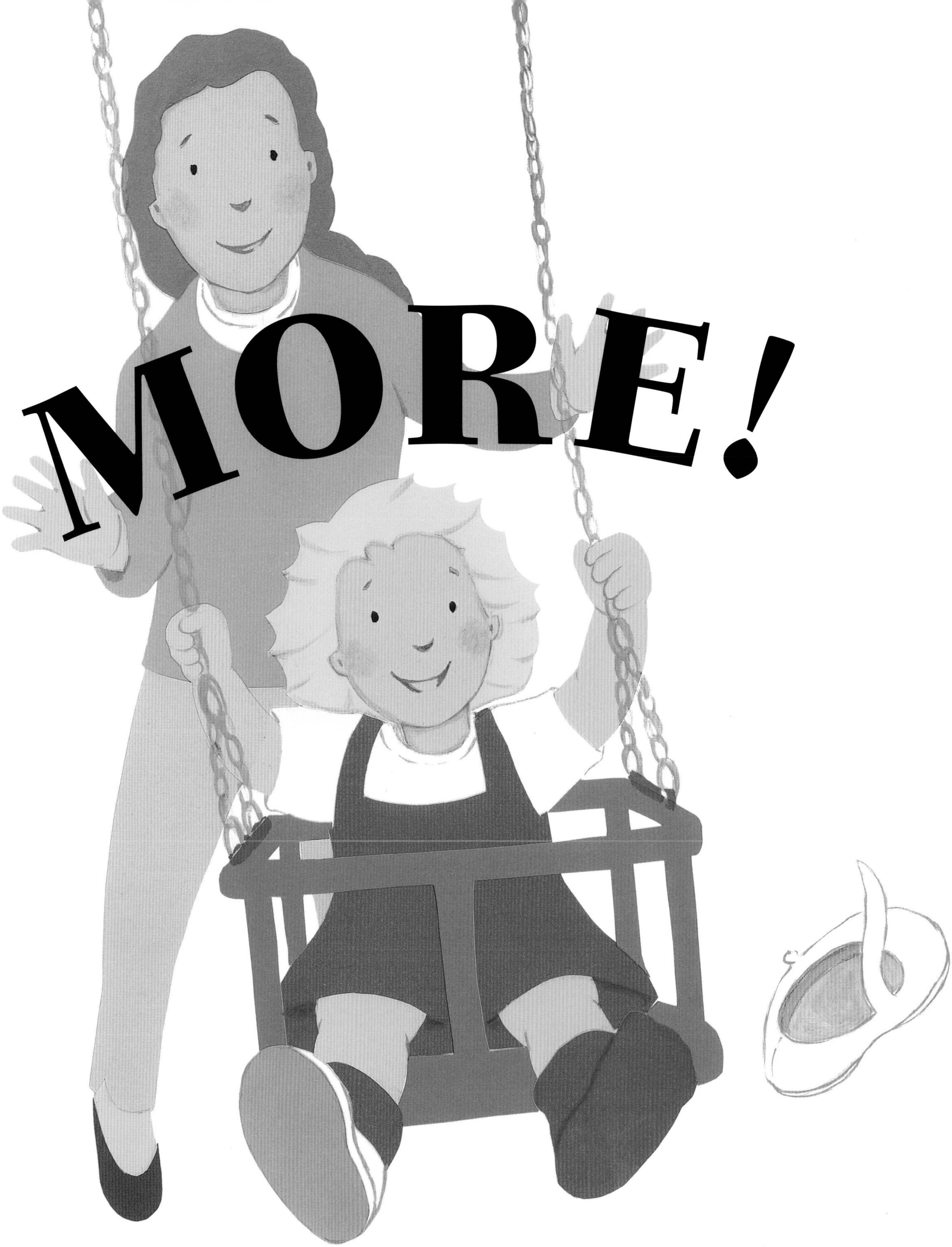
MORE!

Come on!

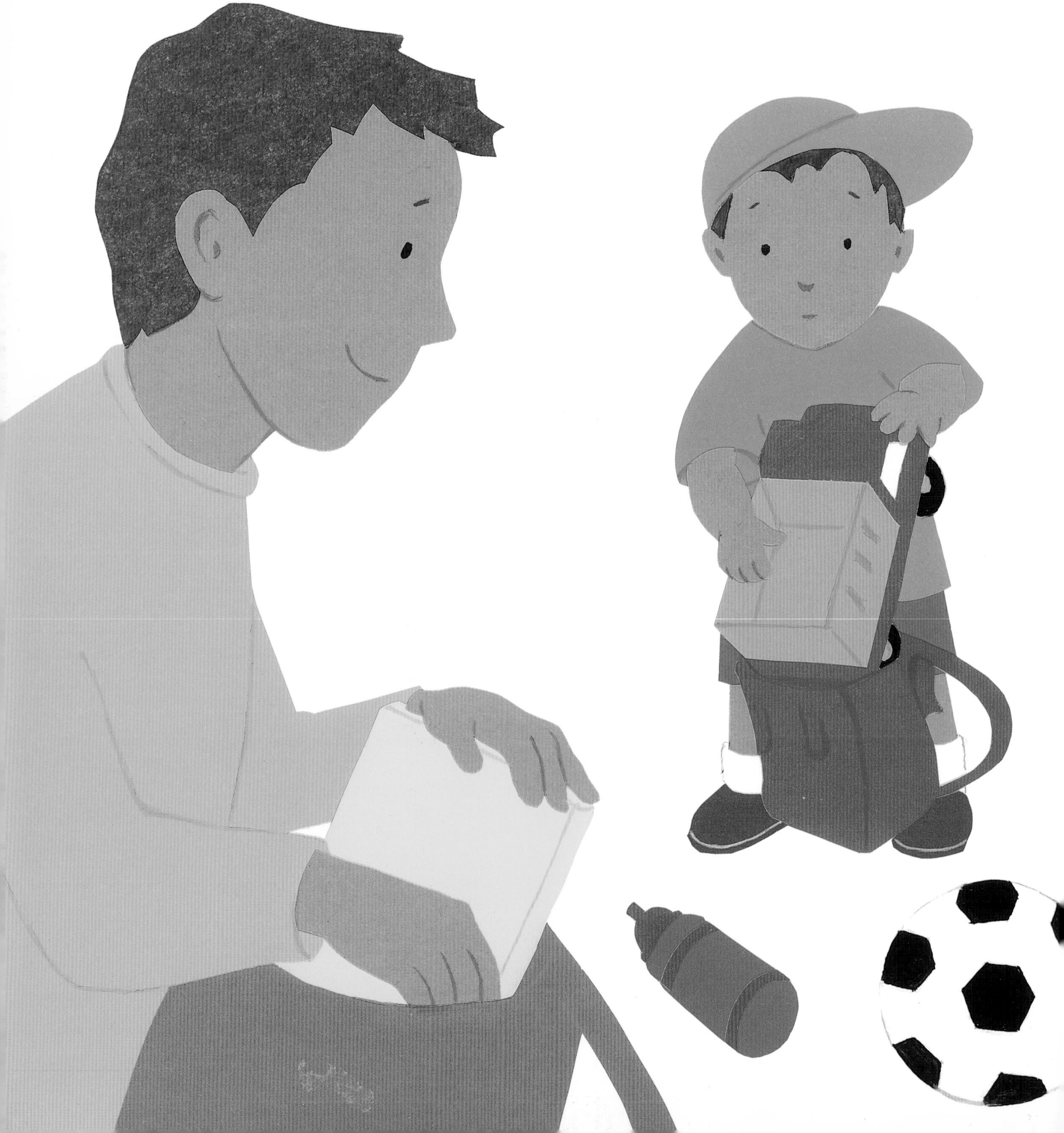

Where's Teddy?

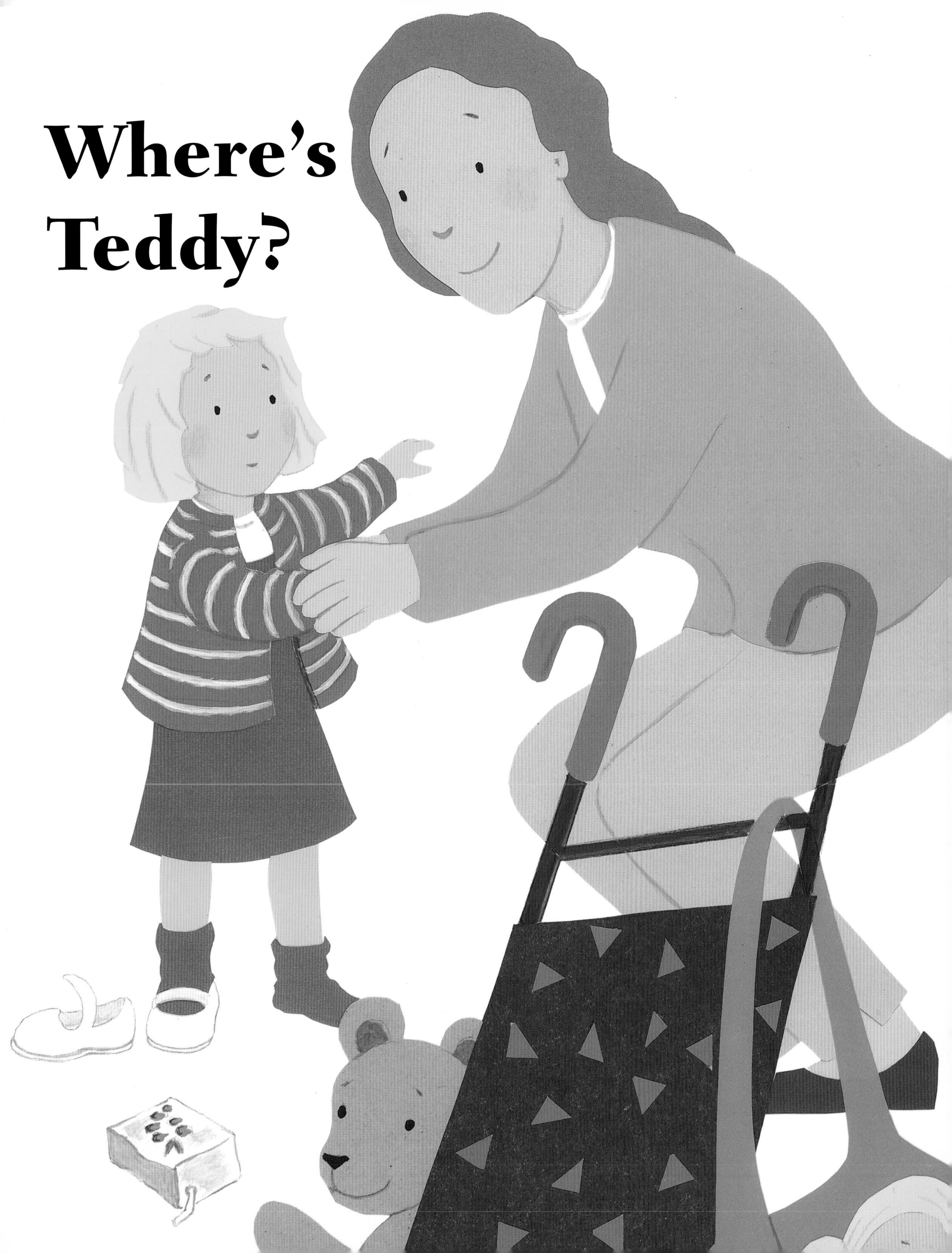

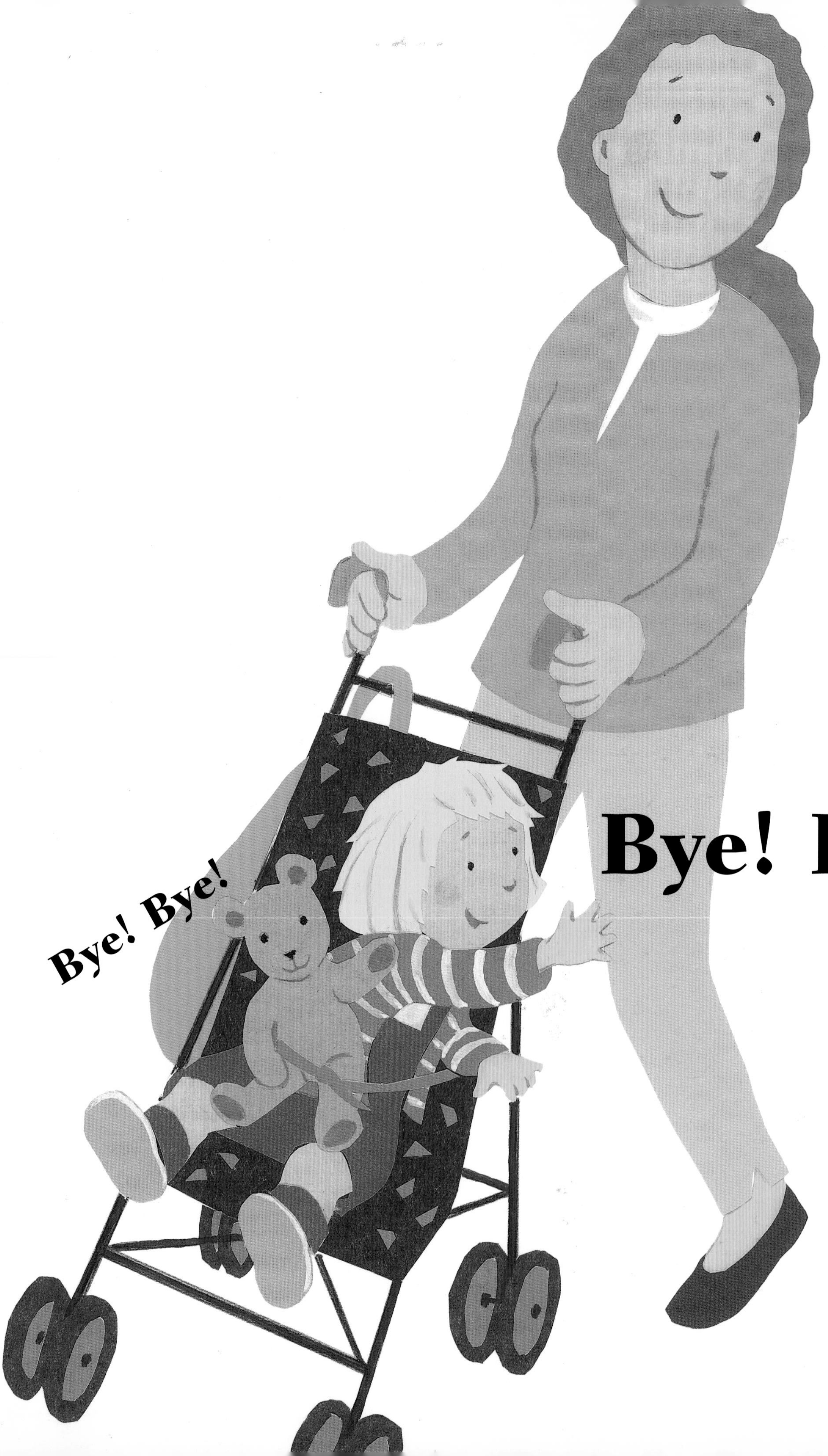

Bye! Bye!